P9-EJU-302

HEADQUARTERS D.I.A.
DINOSAUR INTELLIGENCE AGENCY
OFFICE OF SPECIAL INVESTIGATIONS

INVESTIGATION REPORT

SUBJECT: SECURITY BREACH

CLASSIFICATION: TOP SECRET

CLASSIFIED

DATE: 27.09.65 AGENT: D. SMELLY

We have a CODE GREEN situation on our claws. The dinosaur way of life is under threat.

We have recently gained the following intelligence from reliable informants: a young human by the name of WALLACE, a.k.a. "Wally," EDWARDS has gathered photographic evidence that proves dinosaurs never became extinct. Edwards has written up a detailed report (including some very "humorous" drawings) with the intention of submitting it to educational authorities, i.e., his schoolteacher. If this news breaks into the general human population, the privacy we have enjoyed for millions of years could be endangered.

We consider this report to be a security breach of the highest order and suggest an immediate covert response. Edwards' soft spot may well be his pet iguana, Spike. Agents [redacted] and [redacted] are currently investigating, and a surveillance operation is in the works.

We urge all dinosaurs to proceed with caution. Stay away from café patios as much as possible. Do not listen to your music too loudly. Do not wear overly flashy clothing. Try to refrain from hula-hooping and uprooting trees in public. Disguises, especially sunglasses, are encouraged.

There is no reason, however, to panic. You know humans — only a few crazies will believe a story like this!

P.S. EAT THIS MEMO AFTER YOU READ IT.

To Katie, my love,
and to Harriet, Stella Charles and George — W.E.

Acknowledgments

Special thanks to all the great folks at Kids Can Press for making this book possible and to Jane F. for helping a little boy with his project.

Kids Can Press acknowledges the financial support of the Government of Ontario, through the Ontario Media Development Corporation's Ontario Book Initiative; the Ontario Arts Council; the Canada Council for the Arts; and the Government of Canada, through the BPIDP, for our publishing activity.

Published in Canada by
Kids Can Press Ltd.
29 Birch Avenue
Toronto, ON M4V 1E2

Published in the U.S. by
Kids Can Press Ltd.
2250 Military Road
Tonawanda, NY 14150

www.kidscanpress.com

The "photographs" in this book were rendered in watercolor, colored pencil and gouache. The sketches were rendered in colored pencil.

The text is set in Schmutz Cleaned.

Edited by Tara Walker Designed by Karen Powers
Printed and bound in China

The hardcover edition of this book is smyth sewn casebound.
The paperback edition of this book is limp sewn with a drawn-on cover.

CM 06 0 9 8 7 6 5 4 3 2

Library and Archives Canada Cataloguing in Publication

Edwards, Wallace
The extinct files : my science project / Wallace Edwards.

ISBN 978-1-55337-971-3

1. Dinosaurs—Juvenile fiction. I. Title.

PS8559.D88E98 2006 jC813'.6 C2006-900889-2

Kids Can Press is a Corus™ Entertainment company

The EXtinct Files

My Science Project
by
Wallace Edwards

Kids Can Press

Objective:

I was going to do my science project on my pet iguana, Spike. But while I was documenting his behavior, I made a major scientific discovery!

Hypothesis:

People say dinosaurs are extinct. But I can prove that they are ALIVE.

Apparatus:

1. Camera
2. Notebook
3. Sketchpad
4. Pencil
5. Flashlight
6. Sneakiest sneakers

Method:

The first dinosaur found me. I found the others myself. I sneaked out at night to observe and record their behaviors.

I looked like this when I saw my first dino.

Major Scientific Discovery!

Does this guy look hungry? Or is it just me?

Spike

Observations:

HABITAT

Dinosaurs of today have left the leafy, prehistoric jungle and adapted to one made of concrete, brick and asphalt. They live in high-rises and like the night-life. Many dinosaurs especially enjoy meeting in cafés to discuss movies, music, art and crushing things.

Dinosaurs are
BIG tippers!

T. Rex?
(or Tea Wrecks?)

The Urban Jungle

These dinos are discussing their favorite film, *Godzilla Meets Pinocchio*.

Observations:

DIET

Although they sometimes have bad table manners, dinosaurs are good eaters and like almost anything. This dinosaur loves canned food — garbage can food! In this photo, we see him snacking on all the major food groups: rotten fruit, shoes, glass, tin cans and bones.

This dino is playing with his food (see "bad table manners" above).

I hope he finds a breath mint in there!

Junk food

Tricerapops

Some dinosaurs love sweets.
(Sugar often makes them hyper.)

Observations:

GROOMING

Dinosaurs like to look good. Some are very glamorous. They apply makeup with mops, brush their teeth with old Christmas trees and floss with garden hoses.

Nail care is also important to dinosaurs — long nails not only look sharp, they're handy for playing the piano!

This dino is getting a haircut and a back massage at the same time!

Gorgeousaurus

(closely related to Glamorousaurus)

Size 800 Triple E

Observations:

HEALTH AND FITNESS

Whether they are stomping down the street, pulling trees out of the ground or playing a game of catch, dinosaurs spend a lot of time keeping active.

Young dinosaurs can often be found practicing their fossilball skills. If an egg hatches during a game, the bouncing baby gets to eat the referee.

These dinos are natural-born athletes!

This dino remembered to bring his shorts but forgot to put them on!

A crack shot!

A player in the PeeWee Fossilball League

Observations:

ON THE MOVE

Dinosaurs often travel in groups. Other animal groups have special names. A bunch of geese is a "gaggle." A bunch of cows is a "herd." I call a bunch of dinosaurs a "bunch of dinosaurs."

Not all dinosaurs travel together. This lone teenager prefers to get around in his foot-powered hot rod.

Fossil fuel emissions

A BONE-ified race car!

Out and about

Observations:

COMMUNICATION

I always thought dinosaurs could only grunt and roar, but they are actually quite expressive and can sing like you wouldn't believe. Dinosaurs love haunting, romantic songs about tasty plants, damp soil and uprooted trees.

This dinosaur gives an earth-shattering performance.

This dino sort of looks like my cousin Mabel!

Note her eye-catching outfit
and fancy footwork.

Observations:

MATING AND OFFSPRING

When we studied birds, I learned that the males use their bright feathers to attract a mate. But dinosaurs are different. It's the females who attract a mate by wearing bold patterns and dancing by moonlight.

The male dinosaur helps to look after the babies when they hatch.

This baby is going to need one BIG diaper!

He's got his father's claws.

Observations:

DEFENSES

Some dinosaurs are super strong and powerful. They help keep other dinosaurs safe.

When not mending his sweaters, this dino-cop is on the lookout for bad guys and bullies (his favorite snack).

Leaping lizards! It looked so much better in the store.

Don't call this dino spineless!

Looking SHARP!

Observations:

EDUCATION

People think dinosaurs have small brains. Not true!! Dinosaurs study lots of things, like philosophy, physics, geology, music theory and flower arranging.

PLATO
Dinosaurs can even read upside down!

This proud dinosaur has graduated at the top of her class. (I think she ate her classmates!)

Future DEANosaur

Observations:

OCCUPATIONS

There are all kinds of jobs for dinosaurs: doctor, lawyer, skydiving instructor, hot air balloon-filler, botanist, ventriloquist, cheese inspector ... But many prefer the traditional role of traveling musician or banker.

Groovysaurus
(also known as Hippiesaurus)

This dino reminds himself that time is money.

Observations:

RECREATION

Dinosaurs have many different hobbies. Some like to roller skate. Others prefer hula-hooping or even yodeling.

This daredevil does everything at once, including one-handed shoelace tying. Some grown-up dinos call this multitasking, but he calls it fun!

Let the good times roll!

This skate is the same size as my mom's car.
Skydiving is also a popular pastime.
Look Out Below!!!

Conclusion:

My research clearly shows that dinosaurs ARE alive — and doing very well! My report proves that they have evolved

- To be very smart
- To be hardworking and playful
- To be caring parents and responsible citizens
- To enjoy the urban jungle, especially at night

They also LOVE a good party!

Party crashers!

One other thing is for certain: dinosaurs are very shy and guard their privacy fiercely. This explains why they have kept their culture a secret from us. Who would have thought that their "extinction" was just a big cover-up? It has to be the greatest hoax of all time ... Dinos really ARE clever!

Thank you for reading

Dear Ms. Walker,

I worked very hard on my project. I typed it all myself. I proved that dinosaurs are ALIVE!! I even had photographs! But when I got up this morning, this was all I could find. I think the dinosaurs ate my homework.

Wally

P.S. Does this mean I get an F?

my report.